Feelings in Three Acts

Feelings in Three Acts
By Shauna Cesar

Shauna Cesar
2020

First Printing: 2020

ISBN 978-0-9959352-4-2

Shauna Cesar
www.shaunacesar.com

Special discounts are available on quantity purchases by corporations, associations, educators, and others. For details, contact the publisher at the above listed website.

U.S. trade bookstores and wholesalers: Please contact Shauna Cesar Tel: (403) 869-5868or email **books@shaunacesar.com**

Dedication

To everyone who has stood beside me and helped me get through the tough times and back on the track toward achieving my goals.

To my love, my husband, my life; Andrew. Thank you for always being there and giving me the knowledge that I can faulter and your support never will.

To Meghan my friend who is always listening even when it's tough and I'm not listening back.

To Mom for being all you are and helping me be all I am.

I am eternally grateful for you all.

Contents

Act One

Calm

Smooth
Clear sky's
Never ending fields
Star-filled inky night sky
Alone

Pain

Hurt
Nerves screaming
Frantic heart pumping
Wishing for eternal release
Agony

Brave

Fearless
Full throttle
Scared of nothing
Victory in the end
Endure

Panic

Anxiety
Unknown threat
Possible danger approaching
Unease bubbling deep inside
Alarm

Engrossed

Absorbed
Enthralling sights
Showing true focus
Attention on what matters
Preoccupied

Love

Devotion
My weakness
Wholehearted pure feelings
Yearning from deep inside
Desire

Curious

Learning
Gaining knowledge
Taking everything in
Soaking it all up
Inquisitive

Joy

Thrilled
Feeling good
More than happy
Laughing from deep down
Glee

Irritated

Vexed
Driven mad
Got my goat
Rubbed the wrong way
Goaded

Kindness

Compassion
Warm hug
Quick to defend
Reliable and steady support
Tenderness

Hostile

Vicious
Hate filled
Biting painful words
Fire in my eyes
Aggressive

Lost

Astray
Gone adrift
No way back
Unable to be found
Vanished

Annoyed

Miffed
Feathers ruffled
Hackles are rising
Got my dander up
Galled

Frustration

Vexation
Wrong way
No longer satisfied
Can't turn it around
Resentment

Bitter

Begrudging
Feeling spiteful
Burned once before
Sour outside and in
Resentful

Anger

Irritation
Feeling provoked
Explosion is eminent
Blood is rapidly boiling
Fury

Ashamed

Rueful
Feeling bad
Does anyone know
History can't repeat itself
Guilty

Sorrow

Sadness
Soul crushing
God it hurts
The edge of misery
Regret

Depression

Misery
Black hole
More than upset
Dejection at its finest
Hopelessness

Alone

Single
By myself
No one else
In a dark hole
Solitary

Accomplished

Ingenious
Highly skilled
Feeling very gifted
On top of it all
Formidable

Empty

Hollow
Lacking sincerity
Echo chamber inside
No direction to follow
Aimless

Pleasure

Fun
Exceeding happiness
Looking for fulfillment
Delectable to the senses
Indulgence

Disgust

Revolted
Grossed out
Nausea is rising
Want to throw up
Offended

Proud

Pleased
Feeling important
Set standards reached
High opinion of myself
Satisfied

Weary

Spent
Dog tired
Craving my bed
Asleep on my feet
Drained

Lust

Desire
Unwavering urge
Wanting it all
Can't see anything else
Covet

Want

Crave
Lust after
I see you
Set in my heart
Need

Shy

Timid
Feeling unconfident
Habitually self effacing
Fearful around other people
Meek

Nervous

Edgy
High strung
All muscles tensed
Scared of my shadow
Skittish

Insecure

Unsure
Passive conversations
Shrinking in place
Biting to the quick
Hesitant

Jealous

Desire
Recent acquisitions
Greedy green-eyed monster
Begrudging you what's yours
Resentful

Free

Unbound
Without ties
All for myself
Nothing holds me down
Liberated

Envy

Jealousy
Greener grass
Want what's yours
Discontent in my life
Spite

Angst

Worry
Not sure
Sense of foreboding
No escaping the trepidation
Unease

Bored

Humdrum
Feeling weary
Lacking any enthusiasm
Living sameness every day
Monotony

Act Two

Cuddled deep inside
At peace with the world
Loving the serenity
Making the most of the quiet

Pulsating continuously
Aching deep inside
I want it no more
Now is the time

Boldly leading
Razing your enemies
Armies will follow
Voices singing praise
Everyone rejoices

Propelled forward
And held back
Never knowing
Is it safe
Calm evades

Enveloped in the folds of interest
Never wanting to escape
Going deeper
Reality melting away
Only one thing matters
Scared to look away
Suspended in one subject
Everything else wants attention
Diversions that don't work

Lingering lustful energy
Only one in the world
Very intense heartbeat
Eternity inside

Child like wonder
Undeterred quest for information
Requesting even more
Investigating every meaning
Open to all experiences
Using all my senses
Sorting through what I've learned

Jubilant feelings
Overcoming me
Yielding to happiness

Irked by everything
Repressing anger
Rankled and ruffled
In control but barely
Taunted and teased
Almost at my limit
Testing my last nerve
Enraged by the end
Driving me around the bend

Keen to help
In your time of need
Never a mean word
Determined to keep the bad away
Nice to a fault
Eyes full of warmth
Sometimes your rock
Simply there

Hissing objections
Opinion stated strongly
Spiteful dismay
True to my anger
Ill-will expressed
Life filled with storms
Everyone odds the enemy

Listless in a sea
Of loneliness and despair
Seemingly lifeless
To those around

Almost enraged
Nerves are shot
Needled to the point
Of distraction
You're under my skin
Exacerbating my ire
Displeased with it all

First in the air
Resentment takes over
Unable to change it
Stumbling blocks surround me
Tasting like defeat
Rejection and loneliness
Abandoning all hope
Tired of the reasons
I am over it
One thing left to say
No more

Behaving like a fool
I'm not that easy
To manipulate
To take advantage of
Everyone who tries
Regrets it

Appalling behaviour
No one of importance
Got under my skin
Exasperating consequences
Rage rising again

Afraid of the consequences
Something could have happened
How did this come about
All for nothing
Mistakes were made
Everything has ended
Doubt in my future

Sadness filled eyes
Overwhelmed with grief
Regretting every decision
Remorseful in the end
Outcome was devastating
Wishing to turn back time

Deep inside my core
Everything is a darkness
People must never see
Repress anything negative
Endless struggles exhaust me
Something feels broken
Sucking all my energy
Invading my soul
Only those closest to me
Need to know the truth

Adrift in a fog
Life's losing meaning
On my own
No one around
Endless nothingness

Adept at everything
Consummate leadership
Completed every goal
Outstanding results
Moulding the future
Pleasantly moving forward
Life is rewarding
Impressed with the surroundings
Skills took over
Heights were reached
Experience acquired
Determination prevailed

Everything feels grey and bleak
Meaningless encounters
Purpose is gone
Today, tomorrow, and yesterday
Yearning for something more

Purposeful actions
Lust filled eyes
Encouraging nod
All or nothing
Seeking gratification
Under your weight
Radiating with heat
Engulfed in the experience

Deep feeling unease
Inner feelings surfaced
Shocked at the approach
Guarded in the response
Under the surface
Stomach is souring
Turned off

Positively glowing
Reveling in accomplishments
Overjoyed with myself
Unbelievable feeling
Desired results are satisfying

Worn out
Exhausted thoroughly
Almost done in
Rest of it's me
Yet I continue on

Longing for it
Urgent need
Strong pull
Taking over everything

Wishing for something
Anything more than I have
Necessity demands it
Truth filled with yearning

Shrinking into myself
Hoping to fade into the background
Yearning for confidence

Not sure what's safe
Easily agitated
Re-evaluating all choices
Varying degrees of regret
Overly sensitive
Unease in uncertainty
Strange to those unknown

Inhibited by self consciousness
Never forthcoming
Shyness radiating off me
Everything seems scary
Contrary to what I'm told
Uncertain with decisions
Relationships are hard while
Envying your confidence

Judging by appearances
Envious of what you have
Admiring from afar
Level head waning
Over reaction approaching
Underlying issues
Suspicion laid upon you

For once it's me
Relinquishing nothing
Ever the optimist
Eternity awaits

Everything I want
Never comes to me
Volumes of good luck
You receive instead

Anxiety toward the world
Not knowing why
Guessing the outcome
States of unease
Totally distressed

Blandness surrounds me
Overall lacklustre
Repetitive days
Endless greys
Dissatisfaction with this

Act Three

Calm

At ease in my skin
Bothered by nothing
Capable of inner peace
Deep relaxation
Feeling no ripples

Pain

Accidental injuries causing
Battered and broken bones
Carefree days are over
Devastated with the feeling
Of hurting all over

Brave

Approaching my enemies
Battleground ahead
Comfort in my confidence
Demonstrating strong leadership
Unfaltering by fear or insecurity

Panic

Almost sure
But maybe not
Can't find the reason
Dread's creeping in
Why won't it stop

Engrossed

Absolute attention given
Becoming fully enthralled
Can't look away
Don't really want to
Feel it consuming me

Love

Always by your side
Because you are the one
Can't think of life without you
Devotion that's never ending
My heart, my soul, my everything

Curious

All about gaining knowledge
Breaking through the unknown
Cryptic meanings becoming clearer
Discovering the true meaning
My life is full of new opportunities

Joy

Amazing warmth inside
Blissful on my happiness
Content in myself
Delightfully rejoicing
Radiating from euphoria

Irritated

Aggravated by your actions
Bothered by your words
Can't find the patience
Don't piss me off
Why does everything wind me up

Kindness

Almost saintly
Betrayal is unheard of
Consideration for others feelings
Distress when others hurt
Treating everyone with care and respect

Hostile

Antagonistic in demeanour and speech
Bordering on wrathful
Confrontation is unavoidable
Dead set against anything
Thrusting fingers in your face

Lost

Adrift in yourself
Belonging nowhere
Can't reach out
Destined to be alone
No end in sight

Annoyed

A little angered
By your maddening
Callous behaviour
Driving me crazy
Wishing to be left alone

Frustration

Another set back
Bitterness seeps out
Can no one see
Discontentment fills me
Nothing is going the way I planned

Bitter

A spiteful little man once said
Be careful who you trust
Careful who you believe
Dangerous times are ahead
When you let another in

Anger

Annoyed with the world
Building inner pressure
Can't control my words
Displeased sideways glances
Red in the face

Ashamed

All for myself
Because of lust
Could have lost it all
Distressed at the thought
Conscience stricken with apologies

Sorrow

Absolve me of my guilt
Bring back my happiness
Comfort evades me
Destruction surrounds me
Lost in my own mind

Depression

Apathy over anger
Because anger breaks
Countless barriers erected
Despondency hides behind
Trying to find a way to stop life

Alone

All is blackness
Because no one cares
Can't find comfort
Depressed and companionless
Strong feelings of emptiness

Accomplished

Ability is not doubted
By looking on
Capable of anything
Deftly progressing
Achieved all my dreams

Empty

Abandoned my purpose
Bare and desolate soul
Careful not to seem useless
Dimly participating in life
Nothing behind vacant eyes

Pleasure

All about satisfaction
Basking in delight
Contentment in your arms
Deriving great enjoyment
Lacking a sense of restraint

Disgust

Appalling in my mind
Behaviour that's distasteful
Caused me to shudder
 Displeased with it all
Repugnant results

Proud

Appreciative of my luck
Becoming the best of me
Content with the outcome
Delightful knowledge
In my important achievements

Weary

Awake but shattered
Burnt out
Continue going forward
Dead on my feet
There's no energy left

Lust

All consuming want
Beseeching for more
Crave from deep down
Distractions are ineffective
Wanting it more than my next breath

Want

Allowing an urgent
Broad longing
Crying out with
Desire to possess
Longing for the time I receive it

Shy

Abundantly unsure of myself
Bashful among strangers
Careful not to draw attention
Doubting the sincerity of others
Used to being walked all over

Nervous

Apprehensive with others
Borderline neurotic
Constantly on alert
Determining the consequences
Strait-laced is safest

Insecure

Another compliment received
Belying what I'm told
Confidence evades me
Doubt takes hold
Held back by all I'm lacking

Jealous

Admiring your situation
Bitter feelings creeping in
Coveting what's yours
Distrusting what I'm told
Wondering what I'm missing

Free

All or nothing
Because it's me
Confined no more
Directing myself
Wherever I want to be

Envy

All I deserve never came to me
Bitterness seeing your life
Contrast in our two worlds
Desire for what you have
You stole what I wanted

Angst

Apprehension surrounds me
Before I do anything
Careful consideration happens
Dread constantly lurks
Unfocused but real worry

Bored

Apathy is creeping in
Because lack of interest
Causes sluggishness
Dullness from the routine
Variety in life escapes me